Man's Best Friend

By J. Boote

CONTENTS

Chapter 1

When Terry Smith's mother told him that life was tough and you have to make your own journey, find your own path, he didn't realise it encompassed all aspects of life. He had assumed she referred to deciding on which career to take, perhaps where to live, whether he would want kids or not. He certainly hadn't expected to find himself so many years later deciding on which breed of dog he was more sexually attracted to.

So many choices.

In hindsight, when he looked back on his life, he guessed that it was probably from a very early age when he knew something was wrong. That he may or may not be like everyone else. At such an age that he knew something didn't quite fit in his world but he was too young to understand the how's and why's. He did know that the things he was doing should very probably remain a secret, though—that much seemed pretty obvious even then.

Looking back, he supposed it was wearing his mother's mascara at school. He would have been around eleven at the time because the following summer he would be starting high school elsewhere. Why he felt the need to wear his mother's makeup he couldn't explain even now. He just felt compelled to do so. It was as natural as getting dressed to go to school. He hadn't even started looking at girls or anyone for that matter, either, recalling how he sat and watched a porn movie with older friends and didn't understand why they had the need to go to the toilet every five minutes. Terry could drink litres of Coca Cola and never need the toilet that much. Maybe they all had some weird disease. They kept scratching and rubbing their balls as well and this he found downright disturbing. He would have been embarrassed about that, but they all kept laughing. Then running off to the toilet again.

He stopped wearing mascara when one of the girls at his school asked if he was indeed wearing it and why. He had been shocked that anyone had noticed. It had been shortly after this time that he started wearing his mother's underwear, namely her pantyhose. He liked to lay on his bed completely naked and just sit and stare at himself, again not sure what he was doing or why. Once he got bored with that, he would dress normally again and life carried on. Another major moment in what would turn out to be a rather bizarre relationship with all things sex-related and when he was now around thirteen was when he decided it was rather cool to tie his feet together while wearing pantyhose.

This was a game-changer. As soon as a length of rope or another pair of pantyhose were wrapped around his ankles the tingling sensations began in his groin. He'd squirm and try and free himself, brings his legs up in the air like the girls did in that porn movie he'd seen and this was awesome. And when he decided to tie a thin piece of string around his now stiff cock and had his first orgasm, Terry finally began to understand what all the fuss had been about.

From then on, he was hooked.

He was still hooked now some twenty years later. Hooked to the bed, with his feet tied to the bed railings behind his head with his hairy arse on display for anyone who might care to look and thrusting a dildo almost the thickness of his fist in and out while rapidly jerking off. The red crotchless pantyhose and high heels which was his current favourite attire gave the whole scene that added touch. So important nowadays in a drab, dreary world. And yet, as he lifted himself as much as possible without breaking his back so his cock was closer to his face for when he came, he realised it still wasn't enough. Yes, it was sexy as fuck and the feel of the pantyhose on his body was almost enough on its own to make him shower himself, but there was also a sense of something lacking in the moment. Something that would really take him over the edge, make his whole body shake with the orgasm not just his spasming cock. And he thought it might be the fact it was a plastic cock he was fucking himself with, not a real one. And if—*if*—it belonged to someone or something that just happened to have long claws raking down his back, well, that would be fucking golden.

In the meantime, though, Terry carried on ramming that plastic tool in and out, all eight inches of it, until his cock exploded and he showered both his face and mouth with his sticky cum. Another job well done.

Almost.

As always, once he'd finished, a feeling of disappointment overcame him. He needed more. If it hadn't been for getting caught that time in the field, he could have had more, but the risks were too high. That time he had ran like an Olympic sprinter, desperate to get away and he hadn't dare look back to see if the guy was chasing him. Fuck that. Just keep running until you get home and lock all the doors and windows. Later on, he had seen the funny side of things despite the knowledge that his favourite dog would now be no more use to him. And he had used the experience, his

6

heart still thudding like a mad thing, to fuck himself just a little harder than usual. If he had had the confidence to go to the local gay bar and pick someone up, he would have taken them home and let them do what the fuck they liked to him. Slap, punch and bite him, he didn't care. Would have welcomed it, in fact. Preferably if they had long, sharp fingernails tearing the skin off his back. But Terry had issues with social interaction and no matter how strong the urges to find himself a real dick to suck and fuck on, swallow someone else's cum for a change, he couldn't bring himself to do it. Maybe one day. That or he could move out of this shitty house where he lived and move into another. One where pets were allowed.

Chapter 2

The guy had made a big mistake. He didn't know that yet or he would have kept his mouth shut. Now, Keith was going to shut that and other things for him. Actually, no, more like open rather than close things for him. Yes, he was going to open lots of things on this prick's body. It was a shame because Keith had liked John. Well, not really, but the guy was pretty funny sometimes and always had a joke and a witty comeback down the pub with others that liked to mess with him. John had a big nose and the sexual references were a constant but John could always defend himself with his rapid wit and turn the tables on whoever was making fun of him. When he had suggested to one guy, Mike, that he could simultaneously sniff Mike's wife's underwear while fucking her arse at the same time with his nose, Mike had almost lost said nose. It had been Keith who defended him and when Keith stepped in, everyone backed off. It had made Keith laugh and so he had felt it his duty to save the poor kid. Now, though, John's wit had become his downfall.

He could have just dragged John outside and given him a severe beating, put him in hospital for a couple of days perhaps, but the problem for Keith—and John—was that Keith had self-control issues. In other words, he had no self-control. His rage often got the better of him and it wasn't until it was too late that he managed to stop himself. When the damage was done and very seriously done. He'd already been to prison twice. Once for giving someone a new, extended and enterprising version of their own mouth, slicing it open from ear to ear so that his cheeks flapped in the wind. He'd done that in the guy's own home, in the kitchen, because he had made a joke that Keith alone might be generating enough sales of Viagra to fund the local pharmacist's early retirement. So after slitting his face open, he had then patiently searched the kitchen while the guy bled out on the floor and proceeded to pour salt and vinegar into the wound. It had stung so much the guy had screamed even louder thus opening up the hole in his face more. Keith had had to laugh over that one. Prick.

The second time had been slightly more serious and required Keith to spend seven years in Norwich prison. On this occasion, a guy, Andrew, who Keith had never seen before, in front of everyone at the pub laughed when Keith had stumbled and fallen over while drunk. After getting his nose punched, Andrew had returned the gesture breaking Keith's nose. But Keith had been clever. Rather than tearing his head off there and then, he had left the pub and waited for the man to leave.

An hour later, Andrew did so, on his own, staggering off to what Keith assumed was home. Keith followed. Just as Andrew finally managed to make the key fit the lock, he pounced. Both of them fell into the small house, with Keith landing on top of him, his nose now bleeding once again from the impact. Quickly, he jumped up, kicked Andrew in the balls before he could get up himself and pulled out his switchblade. As Andrew struggled to pull himself up, unaware that Keith had a knife in his hand, he grimaced as the blade sliced across his face.

"Think you can fuckin' hit me and get away with it, you stupid piece of shit? Especially in front of everyone at the pub? The next few minutes of your life are gonna be pain. You're gonna wish you were dead and buried by the time I finish with you."

"No, stop. I…I'm sorry. Don't hurt me. I got a kid. She's only little and she needs me. You've done enough damage, just go. I won't say anything."

"I only just got started, son."

Keith kicked him in the balls again then grabbed him around the neck and dragged him further into the house, until they came to the living room. Whether anyone else was in the house or not, Keith didn't care. And if the guy did have a daughter and she came down and started screaming or something, well, he'd shut her up too.

Sprawled on the living room floor, Andrew's eyes were wild with terror. A scrawny guy, how he thought he could get away with hitting Keith he didn't know. Some people were just asking for trouble. He evidently thought he had balls; Keith wanted to see just how big those balls actually were.

The adrenaline was coursing through Keith now so bad he was shaking. He couldn't have stopped even if he wanted to. Now, he was a man possessed, his body taken over by demonic forces. Forces that demanded suffering, pain and torment. That wanted to see the blood soak into the carpet, hear the cracking of bones, the tearing of flesh. And Keith was only too happy to oblige.

His trademark steel toe-capped boots on, Keith drew back his foot and delivered a heavy kick to Andrew's face, smashing his jaw instantly so the bottom half of his face jutted to the left giving him the appearance of someone severely deformed. The snapping sound echoed around the room. An acrid smell of urine filled the room as Andrew pissed himself. Keith thought he might have shit himself too; that, or the smell of his piss was potent. It made him sick to the stomach, almost making him gag as it wafted up to greet him like an old friend. It made him angrier too. Something would have to be done about it.

And now that he was even more angry than before, it was as if all his senses had diluted, to the point he lost his sense of smell. His eyes were blurred with rage as he glared at the pathetic, shit-stained figure before him. He'd have to learn a proper lesson this one. Keith considered slitting the man's throat, appeasing the demons inside him, so they could watch the blood run, simultaneously with the piss and shit, down Andrew's legs. But no, that would be too quick. Too simple for this guy. This guy was going to suffer a long time.

The man's whimpering was dying down now. Just a pitiful squeak as he tried to drag himself away. Keith kicked him onto his back and squatted down, thinking about where to start. So many ways, so many choices. To start, he sliced through the guy's t-shirt exposing his hairy chest, then ran the blade down the centre, drawing a fine line of blood. An impromptu autopsy occurred to him. He'd always wanted to be a surgeon, be the one paid to cut people open for a living. Or the dead, didn't matter. See what really went on inside. Maybe later. For now, he brought up the blade and sliced off his nipples. Blood squirted into the air as he pressed down on his chest reminding Keith of whales spurting water out through their air hole. It was quite funny. Andrew didn't seem to think so, though, verging on blacking out. To help him wake up again, Keith pulled out his cock and pissed onto his face. He'd had quite a few beers tonight so the stream was endless, steam rising from Andrew's face and chest like a rising mist on a cold, wet field. It did the trick as Andrew spluttered and tried to turn over, impeded by Keith's heavy foot on his chest.

"So you think you got balls, huh? Think you're hard? You wanna know what's hard? I'm gonna show you what's hard."

Keith picked him up and threw him face down onto the sofa then pulled the man's trousers down. Keith wasn't gay, had a girlfriend at home who took care of all his needs and more, but when he had done his first stint in prison, he had learned a sometimes painful lesson. When one needed a fuck desperately, sometimes any hole would do. Some of the cons would have screwed a fucking rat had they been able to catch one. And after six months without a good fuck, when the opportunity presented itself to him thanks to a generous cellmate, Keith had found his cock hardening at the mere thought.

And with a bit of lube to make the job easier, he had soon forgotten the arse he was fucking belonged to a man and not a woman. As long as he didn't stare for too long at the hairs on the guy's back and arse and ignored the deep groans like a dog barking as he pumped him. After that first experience it had become a regular one but of course no one outside of prison would ever know. If they did…

The guy, perhaps conscious of what was coming— literally—tried to squirm his way into a standing position, gargling some kind of pleading gesture through his broken jaw and a mouthful of blood, but Keith ignored him. He thought of ramming the fucker without lube, let the fucker know what it was like to

12

really bleed, but experience had also taught him it might be painful to his own cock as well, so instead scooped up some blood from the puddle on the floor and spread it over the guy's arse cheeks that were smeared in his own shit. Then, for additional ease, he squatted on the floor and rubbed his cock in the puddle as well.

"There, don't say I didn't try to make it easier for ya." And before Andrew could resist, Keith sank his cock into the man's hole.

Andrew gave a muffled groan that would probably have been a scream save for the awkward positioning of his jaw and grunted as Keith rammed him as hard as he could, his balls slapping on the guy's arse.

"This'll teach ya not to fuck with others, or they might fuck with you. You like that, huh? Makes ya horny, does it? I'd cum in your fuckin' mouth but your broken jaw might cut my dick. Shame, that."

He continued screwing Andrew for a while, enjoying the spectacle and the tightness of his hole. His girlfriend rarely let him fuck her arse but when she did she insisted on copious amounts of lubrication first which kinda ruined it for him. Her arsehole wasn't quite as tight-fitting then and she made loads of wet fart noises which also helped to ruin the intimacy of the operation. This guy was starting to do the same, so Keith speeded up, the back of the sofa now banging hard against the wall and after a few more seconds, he rammed into him as hard as he could when he came. Andrew buckled and was shoved forward so that Keith almost fell on top of him when he slipped into the puddle of blood beneath him. Finally, he pulled out his cock and wiped it on Andrew's back.

"Fuck, that was good. I came so hard I'm surprised it didn't fly out your mouth. Must've gone right up to ya throat."

He might have left things at that, but Andrew made yet another mistake. He turned his head and glared at Keith with a look that suggested things weren't over between them. This was his doom.

Keith pushed him over onto his back and peered into the broken man's face. "You testin' me, are ya? Think you're gonna get a little revenge, do ya? Well, fuck you."

He picked up his switchblade from the floor and thrust it into Andrew's eyeball. It made a soft hissing sound as it punctured the membrane, like a gasp. Keith wiggled the blade about, sank it a little further in then dragged it out. It plopped onto Andrew's cheek and wobbled back and forth like a metronome, barely held in place by thin nerves like bloodworms. Andrew thrashed about on the sofa making the eyeball swing harder, until it flew off and landed in the puddle. Keith bent down to pick it up, studied it for a few seconds, then pushed it into Andrew's mouth as far down his throat as he could then punched him under the jaw forcing him to swallow it. For a moment, he thought the man might choke to death on his eyeball but fortunately he swallowed it, his face turning greener by the moment.

"There, not gonna look at me like that again, are ya? Taste good? Like jelly, I reckon. You want the other one?"

Andrew shook his head from side to side, his remaining eyeball bulging, nearly popping itself as though it wished to join its companion. As Keith stood up to admire his work, it occurred to him that this room fucking stank. The smell of the shit that was now drying on Andrew's legs was so pungent it must have soaked into Keith's clothes. He was going to have to change them before he went home. Sarah would be annoyed. It also occurred to him that at some point this guy was going to end up in hospital and answering police questions. Keith didn't want to go back to prison. That couldn't happen. So with no witnesses, no one connecting him to this little incident except Andrew he figured he might as well finish what he'd started.

Stuffing the guy's own eyeball down his throat and making him swallow it had been pretty funny. He wondered whether to repeat the operation. Then the man couldn't identify him if he survived. If he cut out his tongue as well and made him swallow that too— well, that would solve all his problems, wouldn't it? Instead, though, and despite everything, it was getting late, Sarah would start ringing around looking for him and besides, he was hungry. Fucking the guy had tired him out, the adrenaline was wearing off now. Might as well get the job done and go home after changing into some of Andrew's clothes.

So he did the next best thing he could think of.

Filling the guy's mouth with his eyeball had seemed a very fitting thing to do, given the circumstances, so he squatted, not worrying that Andrew might retaliate as he was barely conscious again anyway, and sliced open his ball sack. Thick secretions like snot dribbled out that almost made Keith gag. Or maybe it was cum, Keith wasn't much of an expert on bodily functions or fluids. Curious, he scooped up some of the mess and sniffed it. It didn't smell of anything really, just a snotty, cummy mess, so he wiped it on Andrew's face, picked up his knife again, and slowly, sliced through Andrew's shrivelled cock. The blood really started to flow now. He held it up as though admiring some ancient artifact and waved it from side to side. Disgusting. To think this floppy little thing was so often the cause of man's downfall (and uprising, he thought with a chuckle). People died because of this thing, men were serving life in prison because of it. Some women became rich because of it or exploited man's addictions and obsessions of the little thing to make themselves powerful. Men had been driven mad with lust because of it. It was a weapon of mass destruction and took no sides. Now, laying there in his hand like a fat, dead worm, it was an inconsequential thing. Pointless and irrelevant and pathetic.

Disgusted, Keith forced open Andrew's mouth again and forced it down to the back of his throat. This time, when he punched the man under the chin it didn't go down to his stomach, but remained lodged there, Andrew too weak to spit or cough it out. Then, he cut off the remainder of Andrew's ball sack and stuffed that down there. For good measure, he clamped a hand over Andrew's mouth and waited for him to choke to death. It didn't take long.

That had been seven long years ago and during that stint inside, something had been born within Keith. Something that was as alive and hungry as any foetus born from the womb of a mother. It was rage. Wrath. Utter contempt for any living person that walked the Earth. The slightest glance his way could trigger him. An accidental nudge in the street made him want to cut the person's face open. Being in there for seven long years he had fucked and been fucked by so many cellmates he even questioned his own sexuality right now. Sure, the first thing he did was find a whore on some dark, sleazy corner and fuck her stupid—her arse, of course, because that was what he was used to by now—and he had enjoyed it as much as the first time he lost his virginity at thirteen, yet at the same time, he really didn't want a third stint at Norwich prison. He was going to do his very best to keep his anger issues under control, and so, he found a job at a builder's yard, loading and unloading lorries, a girlfriend and moved into the small bungalow behind the building. Somewhere out in the middle of nowhere almost, just him, his girlfriend and his dog. But even here, he couldn't live in peace. And now, all thoughts about keeping his anger issues in check had flown out the window. Someone had been messing with his dog, who in turn was messing with him and Katie. Keith might have grown accustomed to fucking other men's arses, but when his dog appeared to be interested in his, it was time to put a stop to things. Besides, his dog's cock was too small in the first place.

Chapter 3

Keith remembered it well. Knew exactly when it had first started. It had been the last time he had proper sex with Katie before she left him. He guessed he could understand. The knowledge that someone was coming into their home on repeated occasions and then the reasons behind their dog being loose every other day and what the fucking thing had been getting up to…yeah, it was pretty fucking sick.

It had been just a month after she moved into the bungalow with him. He'd picked her up at some sleazy bar across town and it hadn't taken long for him to understand she was into all kinds of weird, kinky shit. The first sign was when she had gotten drunk on one of their first dates and when they had gone outside for a smoke she had pulled down his trousers and proceeded to give him a blow job. This was fine by him and apparently also fine by the small group of people who were also standing outside smoking. They clapped and cheered as her head bobbed up and down, the sound of her slurping on his dick as though sucking a lollipop. And when he came deep down her throat and she stood up and licked her lips, not the slightest bit embarrassed by what she'd done, Keith realised this girl was special. And it soon became apparent that just having a cock inside her, despite the fact Keith was pretty proud of the size of his, wasn't enough for this girl. This girl needed and craved more.

On the night before the dog started disappearing, Katie was tied to a hook hanging down from a piece of steel chain from the ceiling. And she was upside down. Her hands were tied behind her back and her legs tied to separate lengths of chain so he could spread them at will.

"Fill 'em all," she had told, no *begged* him. "Just like before but harder. Treat me like a fucking slut. And fill 'em all at once. If it fits up my fucking nose, stick it in there. Every orifice, Keith. You know what to do."

Yes, he did know what to do. Admittedly, it was the first time he'd hung her from the ceiling, so that she was swinging around like a dead cow in an abattoir, but it was cool. Her long black hair was tied back in a ponytail so he had something to grab onto and her large, heavy breasts were tightly tied with rope around them, causing her nipples to harden like small rocks. When he flicked them she gave a squeal. When he bit them, she howled.

Fit with a pulley system so he could pull her up and down as required, he lowered it so her face was in line with his now throbbing cock. A teaser first, he gripped it and rubbed it over her face, tickling her lips as she opened wide and stuck her tongue out like a frog trying to catch a fly. In the meantime, with both hands, he spread apart her pussy lips and used his tongue on her pretty much as she was doing on him. She was already soaking wet but for this trick he would need more lubrication so grabbed the bottle and poured generous amounts over her while working it into her pussy and arse with his fingers. She moaned and tried to say something but with his cock in her mouth she was struggling. Then she groaned as his whole hand slipped inside her, slowly working up and down. He'd always wondered what would happen if he kept going further and further. Would his hand push up through her throat, right through her stomach and all the way to the top?

How did that work exactly?

He thought of asking her but didn't want to come across as completely stupid. He then remembered Andrew from years ago. *Should have tried it then.*

"The other one as well," she said letting his cock slip from her mouth. "Both at the same time."

"Yeah, I know, I'm workin' on it. Shut up and suck."

Keith pulled his fist out and grabbed the fist-sized dildo on the sofa. Again, using his fingers first to open her, he then pushed the dildo into her arse while at the same time returning his fist to her pussy. It never ceased to amaze him how women could be stretched so much. He'd seen some pretty large dicks going into cellmate's arseholes in prison that had shocked him, and even he had been dubious about allowing it to happen to him, but this? Then he remembered seeing his sister's baby shortly after she gave birth and realised that miracles did indeed happen. He inadvertently clenched his own butt cheeks meanwhile, though.

As his arms worked like pistons, up, down, up down, his fist and the dildo worked in tandem, this exact scene would return to him some time later as he finally encountered the person he would be looking for. The lengths some people went to, to satisfy their needs. Always looking for more, taking risks, expanding not just their horizons but the various parts of their anatomies. Back when he was a horny teen it had been enough a quick, basic fuck. Even for the girls he had been with. Now, it seemed that unless one possessed a dick the size of a horse it wasn't enough. He thought of the flaccid little thing that had belonged to Andrew.

Soon, there would come a day when men weren't required anymore except as tools to create babies. Then dicks just wouldn't be big enough. That was a sobering thought.

His arms were starting to ache now from the awkward position they were in and he figured Katie must have come herself enough times for him to stop. All that was coming from her mouth were grunts and moans. He pulled out his fist and the dildo with wet slopping sounds and his dick from her mouth.

"You had enough yet?"

Her face was very red, like a tomato. Must have been uncomfortable more than anything else but she had told him she'd done it before and it was his turn to do the same to her.

"Fist fuck my arse."

"What?!"

"You heard me."

Fuck, this woman was insatiable. All he wanted to do was fuck her like a normal human being, but after having that mega-sized dildo up there, plus his fist, he looked at his cock and it almost paled into insignificance. Had something happened to the population while he was in prison? An increase in hormones or whatever the fuck they were called? Looking down at the gaping arsehole was like looking into the mouth of a cavern or some weird fish as it opened and closed, the wrinkles around it like leathery skin. As long as she didn't ask him to piss or shit on her, though. And he wasn't entirely sure she wouldn't.

But, wanting to keep her happy, and slightly grimacing as he did so, he poured some more lubrication into her arsehole then pushed his hand in.

Her arse seemed to suck it in like a vacuum, swallow it up. He only prayed that when he pulled it out again it wouldn't be attached to anything. An intestine or something.

Finally, some ten minutes later, she spat out his cock and said she'd had enough and wanted to be let down. At that point their dog, a German Shephard, came bounding in wagging its tail from side to side as if it wanted to play as well. This scene would also not be lost on him.

"Fuck off," he spat. "Go find a dog to fuck or something."

He untied Katie, her eyes gleaming in ecstasy and raw desire and threw her on the sofa. There didn't seem any point in fucking her now after everything she'd had inside her so he fucked her mouth instead until he came.

"You really get off on all that? It doesn't hurt or anything'?"

"I fuckin' love it! I like to push myself, see how far I can go. You should try it. You might like it."

Keith wasn't going to tell her now that he had tried it and yes, he did like it. Some secrets were best kept precisely that.

It had been the next day when he finished his shift and saw the dog that he kept tied to a long leash was free. Katie worked all day as a secretary, and probably worked on fucking the boss as well he guessed, so she wouldn't have let him go. The biggest issue he had was that the front door to the bungalow was slightly ajar. Someone had broken in.

Not someone to back down from a confrontation, Keith stormed in, hoping he did catch whoever it was still in there. It might cost him another lengthy spell in prison, though, so if they were in there he was going to make it worthwhile. This time he'd gut them. But as he went through the house it was obvious the intruder had fled. What he couldn't understand was that nothing was missing. The TV was there, his stereo system, Katie's laptop. It was only when he checked the drawers beside the bed to ensure the few but very sentimental pieces of jewellery were still there, that he stood back and frowned, confused. All her underwear was missing. He opened the drawer below. The same. All her knickers, bras and pantyhose were gone as was the sexy gear she had hanging up in the wardrobe. Even the dildos and vibrators were missing. All twelve of them.

"What the fuck?" he said slowly.

"What the fuck!" screamed Katie when she came home and he told her. That same night, they piled into his car, after finding the dog and tying him back up again, and went to the sex shop to buy more clothes and toys. Once he had calmed down and was relieved to see nothing of value was missing, Keith had come to see the funny side of things. Someone had been so desperate for a women's sex toys and lingerie they had felt the need to break in and steal it? That was fucked-up.

He wasn't laughing the next day, though, when he came home from working literally two minutes away on the other side of the bungalow behind a few trees and the main office. Because the dog was once again loose and the front door open. And this time when he barged in and stepped into a human turd in the middle of the living room, he roared in disgust and rage.

Again, as before, all Katie's toys and lingerie were

missing, nothing else, but this changed everything. Someone was targeting them, stalking them. Waiting for them to both leave for work, then for some reason untying the dog and breaking in. What kind of sick fuck breaks into a person's home, steals all the woman's sex stuff and underwear then takes a shit on the carpet? Just what the fuck had happened to the world since he'd been away? Everyone was fucking obsessed with sex it seemed, and not the normal type either, because it seemed pretty obvious to Keith that it was a man doing this. Surely a woman wouldn't go to such lengths as to shit on the floor? It had been a pretty fucking big shit as well, splattering the walls when he stepped in it. Women didn't shit like that, did they? For seven years, while he had been giving and receiving cock, the world had turned into a fetishist, sex-craved planet. If it carried on like this, normal sex would become a thing of the past, men wearing women's underwear while they screwed and the women fucking themselves with their fists while taking a dump.

But that was something to think about later. First, find the dog and put him on a longer leash but closer to the door and also a padlock on the leash so the perv couldn't rob him anymore. It might only be Katie's toys and underwear but that was still some expensive shit he had to pay for. And yet, as he wandered around the site looking for the dog, he couldn't understand why the need to free the dog anyway. The perv could have just walked around him to get in the house. Why let him go?

The answer came just a few days later.

He had taken to coming to check on the house as often as he could during his shift. Hopefully to catch the perv red-handed and beat the shit out of him. Then tie him up somewhere in the house until his shift finished and he could resume killing him. But whenever he did the door was locked and the dog still there. Beyond the bungalow was a huge field that sloped upwards so he couldn't see too far but he always wandered a little to see if the guy was spying, biding his time, waiting for Keith to return to work. He never saw anyone. And yet, every time he finished his shift, he would say goodbye to his colleagues, head around the back and there it was—same scenario. The front door open and the dog missing. Katie's stuff missing.

A large padlock was fixed to the dog's collar and there was no way it could pull it off itself, so someone was doing it on purpose. Each time the dog would come running back to him, tail wagging like a mad thing as though it was the happiest dog alive. And Keith soon found out it was. He'd told his colleagues what had been going on who found it pretty amusing. He hadn't mentioned the sex toys, though, only her underwear and the dog. But the following morning, he told his boss he was going home to check again while on break. It was ten in the morning, most people still half asleep, the only thoughts on their minds getting through the day as quick as possible and getting home or to the pub.

Assuming all would be okay, he headed around the back of the builder's site towards his bungalow when suddenly Keith stopped. He stared ahead of him for several seconds trying to understand what his eyes were seeing. Because it didn't seem possible. Not this early in the morning. But there was no denying what he was witnessing up there on the field in full view of anyone who happened to come strolling past. Like Keith.

A man, perhaps in his early thirties with long, black hair was on his hands and knees in the field, his trousers and underwear around his ankles, stockings and suspenders on his legs—Katie's stockings and suspenders—and Basher, his dog, with his front paws raking the man's back while he panted and fucked the guy on the floor.

As Keith stared at the panting dog and the semi-naked guy, he thought of him breaking into his home, shitting on his floor, stealing Katie's toys, the dog that had been free from its leash for a week now every single afternoon. He thought about Katie hanging upside down from the living room ceiling while he fist-fucked her and filled her with various contraptions, the dog coming in wagging its tail like it was doing now. This guy wore Katie's lingerie then allowed himself to be fucked by a dog, then probably fucked himself with Katie's toys later on in the evening. He wondered how big a dog's dick could be when hard. What satisfaction could be obtained by being fucked by something so small? At least if he fucked the dog and not the other way around, he might even be able to understand in some abstract way. Did he suck the dog off as well? Turn him over onto his back and do a 69'er with him? Dress the dog in Katie's stockings? Did he swallow…No, Keith couldn't even begin to think about that one.

For the last few nights, it had been raining and so they let Basher stay inside with them. Just lately, he had developed a tendency to try and fuck them, jumping onto his or Katie's back when they were kneeling on the floor for whatever reason and banging away at them until they threw him off.

Keith felt sick.

Keith's hands clenched into fists.

Bile rose to his throat.

Keith screamed at the guy that he was going to fucking kill him right now and shot off after him.

The guy wasted no time. He jumped up, pulled up his trousers and bolted. He was already halfway across the field before Keith even got onto it. As he watched the man run off, Basher came bounding over to him, still with a hard-on, wagging his tail, happy as could be.

"You can fuck off," muttered Keith.

He watched the man reach the end of the field and disappear. Keith made two decisions that day. From now on, the dog was staying outside regardless of the weather and the man that had been breaking into his home was going to die.

Chapter 4

Dave left After Midnight, a popular gay bar in the area and headed home. Tonight, he was heading back alone and this was disappointing. He had been hoping to pick someone up, take back to his place and maybe smoke a little weed and take a few lines. He'd bought a bag of coke precisely for that reason but it looked like it wasn't going to get used which was a shame. It would have to sit there in his drawer unattended until he did pick someone up. The only time he used coke was during sex. It made it so much more intense, prolonging the orgasm until both he and whatever guy he'd picked up were panting with exhaustion. And their arses throbbing like a bomb had just gone off up there.

Looked like he'd have to take matters in his own hand again. Literally. Somewhat dejected—it was Friday night, after all, and he'd been looking forward to this all week—he arrived at his apartment and opened the door. He stepped in and was suddenly thrown across the hallway, landing in a heap on the floor. Before he even had time to turn around and see what had happened, an arm gripped him around the neck, choking him.

"Gotcha, you sick, pervy fucker. Like fuckin' dogs, do ya? We're gonna see what else you like fuckin'."

Keith grabbed the keys off him and checked the label. 1A. Downstairs, then, even better. He dragged him along the floor until he found the guy's door, opened it and bundled him in. He turned and locked the door behind him.

"Well, well," he said and turned to face him, "I thought I met some sick fuckers inside, but you really take it to the next level, don't ya?"

"Wh-what are you talking about? Who are you? You're mistaking me for someone else?"

"No, I'm not. I recognise that face, that hair makes you look like a fucking woman. Did you fuck yourself with my girlfriend's dildos after you let yourself be fucked by my dog? How's that feel, having a dog's cock in you?"

Dave tried to answer but before he could, Keith stepped up and kicked him with his steel toe-capped boot in the balls. Dave doubled over, the air kicked from his lungs. Instead of a scream all he could manage was a grimace and a weak gasp. Keith pulled his switchblade out.

"Get undressed."

"No, please," managed Dave. "I haven't done anything. I don't know what you're talk—"

Another kick to the face shut him up. "Gonna make it even more difficult, are ya? Alright." Keith squatted and sliced through his t-shirt, then kicked off the man's shoes and pulled his trousers and underwear off.

"Not wearing my girlfriend's underwear? Where is it? And her toys? You like the fist-sized one the best, huh? I bet you really split your arse on that one, didn't ya? Ride it like my fuckin' dog rode you. Did you swallow his cum?"

Dave was sobbing now, shaking his head, trying to drag himself from the towering figure above him. He looked like he was going to either puke and faint at any second. But Keith remembered these were apartments and if he did scream, someone might call the police. Couldn't let that happen. He straddled Dave and stabbed him in the mouth. So hard the blade smashed through the man's teeth and buried itself in his tongue. There, that would shut him up for a bit. Keith wiggled the blade trying to free it and with it came half the man's tongue stuck to the blade. It looked like a bug he had just skewed.

"Ah, for fuck's sake," groaned Keith. Dave had pissed and shit himself just like the guy all those years ago. Keith winced at the acrid stench and quickly jumped off to avoid getting any on himself. A thick puddle of yellow-brown liquid formed beneath him, while blood filled Dave's mouth and ran down his chin.

"I just want you to know that you deserve what you got comin'. What you did in my living room, shittin' on my floor, fuckin' with my dog, stealin' my girlfriend's stuff—you're fuckin' sick. People like you don't deserve to live. You deserve to suffer."

Dave was barely conscious, holding his bleeding mouth, spitting out teeth and blowing blood bubbles. Keith thought about stepping in the guy's shit in his house, throwing away the boots rather than cleaning them. How Katie had had to scrub that carpet but never quite removing the brown stain. They'd bought a rug instead to cover it. Keith unzipped his jeans, pulled them and his underwear down and squatted over Dave's face. Keith had had a curry for dinner and had ordered the spiciest, hottest chicken curry they had as part of his preparation for tonight's festivities. It had taken a few weeks but after haunting the gay bars around the village he had finally found him. The one with the long, black hair. Hadn't been too hard, either. There were only two gay bars and with the kind of fucked-up shit this guy was into, he was guaranteed to frequent them regularly. Katie had already left, gone back to her mother's to live, sickened by what had happened, so unfortunately, she wouldn't get a chance at revenge, but that was fine with him. He already had another girlfriend. She liked it rough, too. He did find it quite weird that Katie had no qualms about giving blowjobs in front of crowds, and having her arse and pussy simultaneously fucked while hanging upside down but couldn't stand to be around a dog that tried to fuck her. He was rapidly coming to learn that some people seemed to have double standards when it came to sex.

Keith pushed as hard as he could, gritting his teeth and heard the first plops as he shat on Dave's face. Then the main course came all the way out and landed with a satisfying splatter in Dave's broken mouth. Eating the curry had been a stroke of genius. It stank like the sewers of hell had blocked up and overflowed onto Earth. As though the chicken in the curry had been rotting in the sun for several weeks before cooking it. Even Keith coughed and spluttered as he wiped his arse on Dave's shirt and pulled his trousers up again.

Dave seemed to be barely conscious of the fact he had a huge turd sitting in his mouth. It looked like a rat trying to burrow its way in.

"Right, that's that taken care of. You shit on my carpet, you get your comeuppance. Now for the rest."

With Dave immobile on the floor, he searched the small apartment for Katie's stuff. This guy wanted to fuck dildos that didn't belong to him, he'd make sure he fucked them good and proper. He was surprised and disappointed, though, not to find them. Just a drawer full of condoms of varying colours and flavours, a few magazines and the guy's own dildos, some of which were pretty big. Not as big as Katie's had been, but still a respectable size. He grabbed the biggest with the tips of his fingers, grimacing when he saw the stains on it. The fucker hadn't even bothered washing it after the last time using it. When he finally identified the guy as being the one, he had spent a couple of nights planning on what he was going to do to him. He wanted this one to be long and drawn out. If it meant a couple of years in prison, then so be it. Keith didn't care anymore. He was coming to the conclusion that those inside were less fucked-up and twisted than those on the outside. In prison no one asked for their arseholes to be fist-fucked. It was a quick fuck and that was it. Or a blowjob. Like the good old days.

But now that he was here he decided to make things up as he went along. He recalled something he'd been thinking when he had half his arm up Katie's pussy and decided to see if it was true. He wasn't sticking his arm up this guy's arsehole, though, no way. He threw the dirty dildo on the floor and picked up an item he'd spotted earlier, then headed back to the living room. The guy had managed to spit out most of the turd in his mouth and seemed to be coming around a bit. Good. No fun if the guy was unconscious and not able to feel anything. He kicked him onto his back, wincing again at the man's stained legs, lying now in the stinking puddle. Then, he kicked his legs apart and squatted.

"Right, let's see if it's true or not."

Keith took the broom handle and rammed it up Dave's arse. He kept pushing, wanting to see if it really did come out of his mouth or not, but when the handle was roughly halfway inside his body it jammed. It had to be near his chest by now, surely. He stood up and kicked the broom. It edged another inch or so. He thought he could see a bulge in the guy's throat so stepped back and kicked it again. Then again and again, until…

"Holy shit, it fuckin' worked! That is fuckin' amazin'!"

The broom handle was now poking out of his mouth, covered in blood and slimy shit, Dave choking as he feebly tried to push it back down. It was true then. Keith couldn't believe it. One learned something new every day. But Dave was now on the verge of dying and he wanted those last few seconds to be agonising. If they weren't already, which they probably were. He wished he'd thought to bring the dog with him, and it was a shame, but never mind, Keith could be constructive and enterprising when required.

He picked up his knife and sliced open the man's chest as though performing an autopsy. The blade snapped, which was annoying, so he went to the kitchen and searched until he found a butcher's knife, nice and heavy in his hand. When he returned, he squatted beside Dave and swung the knife into his chest, hacking it open. Blood flew everywhere, splattering Keith in the face and chest. Inspired, he continued hacking down until a long, jagged gash was opened, like a crack in the road caused by an earthquake. The broom handle was there which he snapped in half and pulled out, then proceeded to hack into Dave's organs and intestines, leaving the heart to last, hoping it kept beating until he was finished. It smelled almost as bad as the turd in Dave's mouth. Almost being the key word. His curiosity was now satisfied. He had always wondered about the workings of the human being, especially after beating one to a near pulp. It was all laid out for him perfectly organised. But this guy deserved to be found in the manner in which he had lived his life—a fucking disgrace to society. Good job there were people like Keith around to dispose of them. He hacked through the organs, pulling them out and throwing them away like discarded junk, until there was a hollow shell. The intestines were still warm and sticky, reminding him of when he worked as a builder moulding putty to put around the windowsills.

Then, assuming Dave was now dead, he turned him over and did the same, splitting open his arse so it appeared the crack went from his cheeks up to his neck. A new definition of an arsehole. For good measure, he hacked off Dave's cock and scrotum, turned him back again and forced them down his throat. Now, whoever was the lucky person to find him would see what a cock-sucking arsehole he really was. Or had been.

Another job well done, the sick fuck now well and truly dead, he went and found some clothes to change into, putting his in a black sack to dispose of later. It never occurred to him that his DNA was now dribbling around Dave's face, brown and steaming still, but it wouldn't matter anyway. On his way out, he was shocked when a guy was standing outside, about to knock on the door. He caught a glimpse of the mangled body and opened his mouth wide to scream. Keith shut it for him and he collapsed to the floor, his lips gushing crimson all down his chest.

"If you wanna know why, that guy was fucking my dog. I caught him. He paid. You go to the police I'll do the same to you. Got it?"

"B-But what are you talking about? That's my

friend. He's allergic to dogs and cats, can't go near them. What have you done?!"

"What? Really?"

"Yes! He has to take pills every time he goes outside."

"Oh. Fuck."

Keith made a hasty retreat.

Chapter 5

When Terry had been a teenager, and after that first orgasm when tied up, he had directed his attention to the girls. All the other kids he was friends with knew exactly what girls to hit upon and how far they had gone or were willing to go. Joanne would let kids finger her while she jerked them off, Maria did blowjobs, and Karla and Jessica had already lost their virginity. There were rumours that Jessica had already done anal but these were unsubstantiated. So naturally, all the boys were onto those that were more promiscuous. Except Terry. He was turned on when the girls came to school wearing pantyhose. It didn't matter who the girl was or how pretty she was, as soon as they came to school wearing short skirts and pantyhose, that was enough for him. And fortunately, one of them, Claire Robbins, was also on the list of the most promiscuous.

Terry had started chatting to her and it hadn't been long before she had gone back to his house after school while his mother was at work and one thing led to another and both were naked. Except Claire whose pantyhose Terry had torn at the middle so he could rub his hands over it while fucking her. Already at fifteen, he had been getting strange feelings about certain boys in his class but he figured this was some just experimentation thing—he'd read about that in a magazine. So the fact that he had been able to comply with his duties with a girl had come as a great relief. Unfortunately, the next time they screwed when she hadn't been wearing pantyhose had been a complete disaster. His dick had flopped out of her after just a few seconds like a limp sausage and the humiliation had been devastating. The next day at school everyone was calling him Limp Dick Terry.

It was his first and last girlfriend until he tried again a few years later, picking up a prostitute from a nearby bar who, of course, had been wearing pantyhose. He was able to perform again but even then he knew girls weren't for him. Not unless she was wearing a strap-on and girls like that were hard to come across unless he paid for her services. And working a meaningless job in a factory meant he couldn't afford to pay for his sex on a regular basis while paying rent as well. Something had to give. It had been during one such session with a girl he met in a bar, though, that would then change his sexuality full circle. Something he had always thought way too bizarre and pretty fucking disgusting, too. The idea of getting off on it was alien, reserved for the extreme fetishists he sometimes watched on the black market movies he bought occasionally. The ones that not even his local video store had sold before the invent of the internet.

But that was then.

He had fucked with Janet a few times, asking her to wear crotchless pantyhose to make the job easier and when she questioned him about his obsession, he came clean. She already knew about his homosexual tendencies so why not tell her everything? Janet had been fond of a bit of sadomasochism as well, so was hardly a stranger to the quirkier side of sex.

"I do have a bit of an obsession," he told her. "I like to wear it myself when I'm alone. Sometimes with other men who come back to my house or even when I'm alone."

"Really? Cool! So what do you do when you're

alone?"

"I get dressed up and I got a few dildos. Use your imagination!"

"Fucking hell, that is so cool! I wanna see you like it. Go get changed in my bedroom, I got plenty of gear you can wear."

And so he did, choosing the sexiest knickers and pantyhose he could find, then, sensing what was coming, borrowed one of her butt plugs and pushed it up his arse.

"Oh, look at you! So sexy. Come here!"

Feeling only slightly self-conscious, he sat next to her and watched as she ran her hands over his legs and crotch. Then she saw the butt plug sticking out of his arse and giggled.

"Oh, I see. I got just the thing for you."

She headed to her bedroom and when she came back, Terry's eyes bulged. So did his cock after a couple of seconds of its own accord. She was wearing nothing but her red, crotchless pantyhose, high heels and a huge, pink strap-on that bounced up and down as she headed towards him like a missile. Janet got on her hands and knees, pulled out his cock and began sucking for a bit before telling him to stand up and turn over. He complied, the anticipation nearly killing him. With a plopping sound she pulled out the butt plug and threw it away. Seconds later, he grunted as his arse was filled, like taking a shit but in reverse. That thing was fucking huge, bigger than anything he'd ever taken before, even more than the biggest of dildos he had at home. And when she started pumping harder and faster he thought his cock might explode as he frantically jerked himself off. But, when she made him turn over onto his back and fucked him while simultaneously playing with his cock, Terry decided he had finally found what he'd been looking for all these years.

But there was still more to come.

"Now, get on your hands and knees again. What's just happened is nothing compared to what you got coming. You're gonna fucking love it."

Curious, and more than a bit excited, Terry did so, not sure what could possibly be as intense as having Janet fuck him hard with her strap-on. He could have died and gone to Strap-on Heaven right there and then.

"Come here," he heard her say and an inkling of doubt crept in. Surely not? But when he felt something practically jump onto his back, claws like talons digging into his skin and then something furry rubbing against him before a smaller tool entered him, he knew. The Alsatian had been patiently waiting over in a corner, now it was on his back fucking him while its hot breath blew onto the back of his neck.

"What the fuck, Janet?" he cried, tempted to throw the dog off him but not wanting to get his neck torn open at the same time. The dog was pretty fucking big.

"C'mon, don't tell me you don't like it, his claws on your back, furry body rubbing up against you? Granted, it would help if his cock was bigger but I'm hoping to buy a Saint Bernard soon. Can you imagine a fucking Cujo on top of you?!"

As the dog panted and pumped away he did admit it was a pretty raunchy situation he found himself in. Especially when Janet got underneath him and began to suck his cock at the same time he was being fucked. When the dog came, it almost tore the skin off his back. When Terry came, more or less at the same time, the dog still on top of him, he nearly gave himself a hernia.

That had been about a year ago, and he had returned to Janet's on a regular basis. She never bought the Saint Bernard, though, which was a shame and eventually she got herself a steady boyfriend so that particular relationship ended. And unfortunately, his relationship with any dog had recently ended, too.

Now, though, tired of bouncing up and down on dildos he figured it was time for the real thing again. It had been a while. Not too many men were willing to wear pantyhose while they had sex. Why, he didn't know. It wasn't as if he was asking them to parade around town in them, semi-naked for the whole world to see. Hopefully, tonight he would get lucky.

He arrived at After Midnight and sat at the bar as always and ordered a gin-and-tonic. It was getting pretty busy already and wasn't even ten yet. There was a mix of men and women, some dancing in various outfits—latex, leather or hardly anything at all. Terry wished he had the courage to openly sit there in a short skirt and pantyhose like others did. Perhaps a little makeup. Some of the trans women were pretty damn sexy. Hopefully he could pick up one of them if they caught his eye. Who *was* catching his eye was a guy sitting by himself at the far end of the bar. Staring at Terry but not with the look of someone out looking for a date. Terry thought of smiling or waving at him but decided against it. He wasn't looking for a single guy anyway. To celebrate his lucky escape the other day he wanted more. Much more.

Another trans woman entered the club and joined the other that was gyrating slowly to the music. Now this was much better. A threesome would be fucking awesome right now. He raised his trousers slightly to just above the ankle to show off the fact he was wearing pantyhose like they were. Hopefully one or both would notice and come over. He didn't really want to have to take the lead here—he often found himself stuttering and getting tongue-tied and his tongue had much better uses than that anyway. Fortunately, after a few moments one of them headed towards the bar where he was sitting. Tall with long blonde hair, a curvy, slim figure, short skirt and white pantyhose she looked like an angel and perhaps she was. He'd get down on his knees and pray to her as much as she liked if she asked. He'd show her the meaning of true worship with her big, fat cock down his throat. A little baptising of the soul but this time instead of holy water, it would be holy cum he drowned in.

She glanced at him and smiled. Terry's heart beat faster in his chest, butterflies in his stomach.

"Hi," he said, not daring to elaborate further.

"Hello there," she said in a deep voice giving away her real gender. "I haven't seen you here before. And that's a shame, isn't it?"

"I guess so. I'm, umm, I was bored so thought I'd come and see where the fun's at."

"Oh, you certainly found it here, love."

She glanced down and saw he was wearing pantyhose and smiled. "Like to keep it secret, do you?"

"Yeah. For now, anyway. Maybe one day."

"Well, would you like to go somewhere where you don't have to keep it a secret? Somewhere a bit more...cosy?"

"Sure!" he replied, delighted. "I live on my own, anyway if you wanna come back to mine."

"Oh, that sounds very nice. I'm with a friend, though."

"Even better!"

Ten minutes later they were heading out of After Midnight together. Terry was already hard just thinking about what they were going to do. He was thinking so much about all the possibilities and positions they might try, how much he could twist and bend his body into impossible positions like a contortionist. Feel a real cock inside him again—he was getting sick of that damn dildo all the time.

And everything turned out better than he could ever have expected. By the time all three had ejaculated—Terry having taken the full force of it all on his face and down his throat, his arse throbbing like a mad thing—he was exhausted. Spent, like the cum in their balls. Exhilarated was also another good way to describe how he was feeling. All this time he had been messing around with dogs and dildos because of how timid he was, afraid to go looking for others in case of rejection and the first time in months all his fears had been banished in a two hour session of screwing. Terry had never been so happy.

Apparently, the other two were also quite happy as they agreed to return the next night for a repeat performance. Finally, things were starting to go Terry's way.

The next night, he rushed home from work and showered before slipping into his sexiest lingerie yet. A pink slip, pink, lace stockings and suspenders to match the pink knickers and some new high heels he had managed to find that didn't crush his toes when he put them on. A flimsy, transparent dress showed off everything, including the largest of his butt plugs. So when the doorbell rang later that night, he was quick to answer the door, a big, silly grin on his face.

"Hello, fucker. Been fucking any dogs lately?"

Terry's smile died. As did his erection.

Chapter 6

Gorleston was a tiny village surrounded by countryside so the gay population was not large. The entire population only consisted of about ten thousand so the chances of Keith making another mistake were slim. He'd been hanging around the two bars alternatively night after night and had confirmed there were only two gays who had long, black hair. And one of them was now dead. Keith wasn't very good at maths but even he knew that left only one. The guy who was now walking off somewhere with the two trans women. His guy.

In front of his friends Keith was the first to publicly maintain his outrage and disgust at how two people of the same sex could actually have sex, but this, of course, was an act. Secretly, he had his own stories to tell. He didn't give a shit anymore whether he fucked male or female; it was all the same by now. He didn't think he could ever stoop as low as to try his hand with the local wildlife population, though. And by the time he'd finished with this guy, he wouldn't be, either.

He followed discreetly until they reached the guy's home and they all headed inside. Keith desperately wanted to finish the job now, finish what he'd started out to do over a week ago, but this time it had to be right. He could just as easily knock on the guy's door, barge his way in and take care of all three of them, no sweat off his nose, but it wouldn't feel right. He wanted this time for the crime to fit the punishment.

And he had just the right idea.

He returned again the following night. A light was on in the living room and the curtains were drawn, meaning the man was at home. If he had company, so be it. This had to end once and for all so he could go back to living his life. The fucking dog still hadn't calmed down, so he decided that after tomorrow, he was going to give it to his parents as a gift. It was his dad's birthday soon—that'd keep the miserable fucker occupied. He thought he might buy a cat next time.

Keith looked around to ensure no one was about and casually walked down the garden path. He rang the bell and waited. A few seconds later the door burst open and the guy answered wearing the biggest smile Keith had ever seen and the skimpiest, sexiest lingerie he had ever seen. For the briefest of moments, he felt the beginnings of an erection develop until he remembered why he was here.

"Hello, fucker. Been fucking any dogs lately?"

The guy's smile was gone in an instant. He knew exactly who Keith was. He could see it in his eyes. He must have heard about what happened to the other guy on the news. It had been front page news for the last few days. The police described the scene as an abomination. Something that only a monster could have done and had to be stopped immediately. In the newspaper report there had been leaks about the state of the body, a certain broomstick handle found in a compromising position. Fortunately, the police's theory was that it was some hate group that probably had ties to Nazi organisations and the culprits—for surely it had to have been more than one person—no doubt covered in tattoos and openly displayed their hatred for the gay community. Shouldn't be hard to find them, the police said. Keith had no tattoos and his brown hair was curly, definitely not a skinhead which is what the police would be looking for. So for now, he was good. Unlike Terry.

Terry tried to slam the door shut, but Keith was ready for that and had a steel toe-capped boot firmly wedged to avoid such a possibility. He pushed the door open and before Terry could scream or call for help, punched him hard in the mouth. Terry crumpled, as did his lips. With Terry on the floor, he took care of the companions he'd brought with him and dragged Terry into the living room and left him slumped on the floor, whimpering and clutching his broken mouth.

"I guess I'm sorry about the other guy. Wasn't his fault, of course. I fucked up. He didn't suffer, though, if that's any consolation. Well, not a lot anyway. You, though. Now that's a different matter altogether. You are in a lot of trouble, my friend. A whole lotta trouble."

"Who are you? What do you want?"

"I think you know who I am. You know very fuckin' well who I am. You know my dog even better, don't you, you fuckin' perv. I wanna know; exactly how does one get any satisfaction from a dog? All those claws, that fur, smelly breath? I can understand all this, you bein' dressed like that. I'd fuck you myself if I was in the mood. In fact, I might just do that, so I got nothin' against gays, trans, whoever, but a fuckin' *dog*? *My* fuckin' dog?"

"I didn't hurt it. It's just sex. What difference does it make? I wasn't hurting anyone, so please, just go, leave me alone. It won't happen again."

"Damn right, it won't happen again. And yeah, I agree it's just sex. Nothin' wrong with that. We all got our fantasies and fetishes. Fuck, I ain't no saint, but not my dog, man. And shittin' in my livin' room? Stealin' my girlfriend's underwear and sex stuff? They here now?"

Terry nodded, his eyes shifting to a chest of drawers over in the corner. Keith went and opened the drawers and there it all was, Katie's lingerie and dildos. Some of them were stained brown, clearly used but he hadn't bothered washing them afterwards. He took them out one by one and threw them at Terry. It wouldn't be the last time he got to use them.

"Why'd ya shit in my house?"

"I don't know. I don't remember!" he howled, tears running down his cheeks, clearly terrified.

"I stood in that. Your shit was sprayed all over my walls. You got any idea how disgusting that was?"

"Please, I'm sorry."

"You're sorry? Yeah, so am I."

Keith squatted and ran a hand up Terry's legs feeling the smoothness of the pantyhose. Terry flinched. Then, he ran a hand over his cock, squeezing it hard. Terry winced.

"Getting' ready to fuck, was ya? Them two trans from last night? They comin' back again? Were gonna give you a good fuckin'? How about I give you good fuckin' instead?"

He rolled Terry over and saw the butt plug. He pulled it out and rammed it in Terry's mouth.

"Taste good?"

Terry made to pull it out, but Keith stopped him. "Uh-uh, leave it where it is. You know, if you'd just fucked with the dog, I would have left it. Since gettin' out of prison, I've realised things have changed. Things are different. People are more open—in more ways than one. And I can live with that. I got nothin' against you people. You ain't hurtin' no one. What you folks do behind closed doors is no one's business, and that's a fact. But stealin' my girl's gear, shittin' in my house. That's unacceptable and you gotta pay. Breakin' in my house. My girlfriend left me, couldn't handle the fact someone had been breakin' in and takin' her stuff. Fuckin' my dog. So you caused me a lot of stress, friend. Thinkin' about it, fuckin' my dog is the least of it all. Might've done it myself if I hadn't had a fuck for a while."

Terry whined and groaned, trying to defend himself, his face bright red, sweat dripping from his forehead. Keith had to admit, he did look pretty hot and in more ways than one. *Fuck it*, he decided.

"Get up."

Terry slowly pulled himself to his feet. Keith grabbed him and pushed him over the back of the sofa, his arse sticking in the air. He pulled the butt plug from his mouth and pushed it into Terry's arsehole, back and forth, wiggling it about from side to side, then put it back in Terry's mouth. Keith was hard already, now that he could mentally visualise a woman bent there. He pulled his cock out and shoved it forcefully into Terry who grunted in pain or lust, Keith didn't know. Probably both. Either way he was enjoying this himself. Prison had taught him a lot of things, one of which was that one shouldn't judge others without having experienced it first. A lot of hypocrites out there, he thought. And that Terry was wearing the sexy gear made it all the more pleasurable.

Maybe it was because of that it didn't take long for the familiar tingling to start building up. He pulled out

48

his cock, turned Terry over and stuck two fingers in his mouth.

"Here, get some of this. Don't wanna leave no DNA around afterwards."

In the gap between his fingers and the butt plug, he guided his cock in and came hard straight down his throat, then closed Terry's mouth again.

"That's in case you were thirsty. We got a lot of work to do." Then, with the largest of Katie's dildos, the fist-sized one, he shoved it up Terry's arse, then kicked it for good measure to make sure it stayed there. Now that the fun was over, it was time to get down to business.

He wanted this to be just right. Terry had to suffer for all he had done and it was only fair he knew it. He took out his new switchblade and held it up to admire, the blade gleaming in the light. Terry must have glimpsed it because he took out the butt plug and turned around.

"Please, you've done enough. Don't hurt me anymore. I think you've ruptured something."

Keith glanced down to see that yes, blood was trickling from the dildo. Even better, then. "I'm gonna rupture a lot more before I've finished, friend."

Keith took the blade, sliced Terry's cheek then stuck his fingers in and tore it open. It sounded like someone taking a bite from an apple. Terry screamed so Keith punched him in the mouth, teeth shattering. Then he sliced his other cheek and repeated the action. They looked like makeshift windows now on each side of his face. Keith took another dildo and rammed it between the gaps so the business end came out the other side. There, that'll shut him up.

Keith's adrenaline was really kicking in now. He felt good, doing something useful for once. There would be uproar from the gay community but that wasn't his problem. It was a shame, because really they didn't deserve it as a collective but it was this guy that had given them a bad name—he had only himself to blame.

As the blood began to pool on the floor and Terry was swimming in and out of consciousness, Keith made a long incision down the length of Terry's arm, then the other. Next, he turned him onto his back and did the same from the back of his neck to his arse, opening him up. He turned him onto his back and continued the incision up to his larynx not wanting to kill him straight away. It looked like some kind of weird zipper, as though his skin was part of a suit and at any time he could slip out of it. The blood slipped from between the cracks like rainwater rising from a blocked drain. Keith groaned and cursed when the smell of piss and shit invaded the room, somehow finding a way past the dildo. Technically, it should have been impossible, thought Keith. Had he inadvertently created another hole? Now, once again, the floor was covered in a reddish-brown puddle, the acrid stench permeating his nostrils. He hoped it wouldn't deter from part two of his plan.

Terry's breathing was laboured now. He might have been dead already except for the slow rise and fall of his chest. Keith pulled the butt plug from his mouth just in case. He hadn't really done anything to him yet anyway. The incision was barely a scratch. Well, maybe a bit more than a scratch judging by the amount of blood. No problem, though.

"Please, just go," mumbled Terry. "You've done

enough."

His face was pallid. Keith was going to have to hurry things along if he wanted him to be conscious for part two. He made an incision in his balls, allowing the snotty fluid to flood the floor as well. Terry groaned. Then, Keith made the incision in Terry's chest slightly deeper, enough to sink his fingers in, then with both hands tried to open up his chest, as though tearing open a particularly tough sack. It was hard work and wasn't as easy as he thought it might be. Should have brought a saw, he realised. Or an axe or something. Why did things always occur in hindsight? It had never occurred to him it would prove to be so difficult. Surgeons just used a scalpel, didn't they? At least in the movies he watched they did. Oh well...

Just below Terry's throat he made two horizontal slashes, then did the same just above his cock, leaving flaps that could easily be torn open. It would be like peeling off old wallpaper—in some places it came away easy, in others, a little more determination was required. This wasn't a problem, either. Nothing was a problem anymore. Only that fucking smell of shit and piss and blood that was now making his eyes water.

But, the job was now done. Time for part two.

Keith left Terry groaning and spitting blood bubbles on the floor and headed outside to the foyer. His dog and another, a Rottweiler he'd borrowed from a friend, started wagging their tails in excitement and impatience. He'd had them for two days and hadn't fed them hardly anything. Just enough to stop them whining. Now they were hungry.

"Yeah, I know. C'mon, dinner's ready."

He untied them and took them back into Terry's

51

living room.

"There you go, boys, dinner is served. Or you wanna fuck him first?" he said, especially to his own.

But apparently, Basher didn't.

The plan must have worked and evidently the dogs weren't too bothered by the foul, pungent stench in the room either. The Rottweiler growled as Terry—conscious enough to know what was going to happen—tried to drag himself away. But Terry was going nowhere.

The Rottweiler latched onto one of the flaps Keith had opened near his throat and began to tear, pulling backwards as though immersed in a tug-of-war. A sizeable chunk of skin and flesh came away, pinging as it hit the dog on the nose. Basher did the same, clamping its strong jaws on the incision in Terry's arm and thrashing his head from side to side as it tore it off. As Keith had imagined, a long strip came away like a strip of wallpaper. They snarled and chewed and slavered over the fresh meat and wanted more.

"Good boys. Carry on," said Keith, keeping a good distance away just in case.

As though heeding his words, the Rottweiler then sunk its claws into the long incision in Terry's chest, as though trying to retrieve some long-lost toy. It sunk it's jaws in and crunched down on the thick flesh. Terry was barely alive now—in fact, Keith wasn't sure at all—the Rottweiler's head was slowly biting its way through the man's chest, possibly digging for tastier, softer morsels buried inside. Then Basher, as if recalling past events and wanting more, took Terry's flaccid cock in his mouth and tore it off in one go, swallowing the thing without even chewing.

Apparently, Terry was still alive because he uttered a weak groan. He wouldn't be alive for much longer.

Terry's chest finally opened. Keith had read somewhere that if such a dog clamped its jaws on something, a crowbar was required to release them. Keith had no crowbar and didn't want one anyway—he was happy to see the dog bury its nose into Terry's chest and begin gnawing and slobbering over the soft organs. It might have been a heart or lung it tussled with—Keith wasn't sure. They all looked the same to him. He glanced at Basher who was now attacking the man's ball sack. It made Keith wince as the dog shook his head from side to side, trying to pull it off. When it did so, the blood gushed.

And then perhaps another memory surfaced as Basher grabbed the huge dildo in its mouth and dragged it out. The rich odour of fresh waste filled the room once more as though the sewers had opened up.

"For fuck's sake, Basher, not that!" Keith kicked the thing from his mouth. Basher ran after it as though playing a game and brought it back, tail wagging, jaws full of blood and gore.

"I'm not playing. You're here for dinner. Eat!"

As though he understood his master's words, he dropped the dildo and resumed lapping up the blood around Terry's lifeless body. The Rottweiler had better ideas. A mouth full of some stringy organ that dangled like a large sausage, it clamped its jaws onto Terry's throat. A crunching sound ensued as Terry's larynx was crushed and torn open, the dog chomping heavily on it before swallowing. Then it started on his face while Basher finished of some of the intestines.

Within minutes Terry resembled a mangled, mushy,

disfigured mess, completely unrecognizable as a human being except for the hands and feet that remained untouched. It might have been fresh roadkill, a deer or something that had been pulverised by a passing lorry. Terry decided that the job was finally done and with certain precaution, grabbed the Rottweiler's collar and pulled him away, then Basher's.

"C'mon, let's get out of here. Hope you rot in Hell, man. You should have kept your dick in your trousers or at least stuck to fuckin' humans." He spat on his mushy, bloody face and dragged the dogs away. When he opened the door, two trans women stood there, about to knock. They regarded him with surprise then shock when they saw the dogs covered in blood.

"Ya friend's in there. Not feelin' very well so you might wanna look elsewhere for a good fuckin'. He got his arse well and truly fucked this time."

Keith pushed past them, having briefly considered inviting them back to his place, then decided against it. He'd had enough fun for one day already.

Chapter 7

The next day Keith did as promised. He returned the Rottweiler to its owner then took Basher to a dog centre, alleging he had to move away and dogs weren't allowed where he was going. He felt sorry to say goodbye and might even had shed a tear had he been alone. The dog had done nothing wrong at all, had been the victim—like Keith—of a set of bizarre circumstances and had gotten caught up in all the excitement. Keith couldn't blame him. It truly was a mad world nowadays, the kind of things one might have gone to prison for a few years ago now openly talked about and acted out in public or on stage for everyone to see. People openly dressing however they liked with barely an eyebrow raised. And Keith didn't mind at all. Not after everything he'd seen and been through. Once upon a time he might have been anti-everything but not anymore. Live and let live was his new motto.

He decided against getting a cat for the time being, though. With his luck the thing would be all claws and teeth and might bite his dick off in the middle of the night. Or claw it to death. That'd be funny. So, instead he decided a bit of peace and quiet for a while, stay low while the police looked for whatever monster had killed and mutilated the two men. It was on the news all day every day, the scenes of carnage compared to Jack the Ripper's work. It kind of made Keith feel proud being compared to such a legend. Fortunately, the police said they had no leads right now, maybe a radical anti-gay group that they were looking into. The gay community were obviously outraged, planning demonstrations and everyone in the community was also terrified of being the next victim. But unless there was a copycat killer out there, Keith's work was done. Once things settled down, he thought he might revisit the After Midnight bar. There had been a couple of cute-looking guys he'd spotted and well, old habits die hard. He thought he might like to try some of that pantyhose and lingerie on—it looked pretty sexy.

In the meantime, he had browsed the internet, found some weird fetish shit that he found pretty kinky and made him horny. A guy wearing stockings and suspenders while being fucked by a woman wearing a huge, pink, strap-on while another woman sucked him off. Unfortunately, it got a little less sexy when the girls pissed on him. He made a mental note that if and when he tried that, if anyone so much sprinkled him in piss, he'd beat the shit out of them. Some things were best left to others.

He finished at about the same time as the guy in the video, grabbed another beer and decided it was time for bed. Just lately, three days after taking care of Dog Fucker Man, he had been hearing strange noises outside. Scratching at the door as though it was Basher trying to get in. But, of course, every time he went to check there was nothing there. Except for the scratches. It might have been Basher's work before he left but Keith wasn't so sure. That scratching sure as hell sounded real to him, not his imagination or drunken hallucinations. Maybe one of his co-workers was playing a prank. He'd pay if he was.

There was a funny, musty smell about the place, too, these last few days. The smell of sex combined with that of the sewers—a mixture of piss, shit, cum and blood that revolted him and had him spraying deodorant around the house all evening, especially in his bedroom. Maybe it was his subconscious still thinking about what he'd done. Signs of guilt? Well, he had no sensation of guilt whatsoever, subconscious or not. What was done was done. And nothing was going to change it. Maybe it was time to find somewhere else to live. He made a mental note to look into it at the weekend.

Tired after half an hour of jerking off to the video, Keith headed up to bed, making sure all doors and windows were locked. He kept his switchblade under his pillow, too, just in case. A couple of times these last three days he had woken in the night for a piss and the back door had been slightly ajar, as if the wind had blown it open. Keith couldn't remember if he had locked it or not—too drunk to remember. He staggered upstairs and practically fell into bed and was asleep within seconds.

And may or may not have woken a few hours later. He wasn't sure if he was dreaming or not, so pinched himself to make sure he really was awake. It felt as though he was but the scene unfolding before his eyes suggested otherwise. From outside, beyond the closed bedroom door, he could hear panting. As if someone had ran to his house and up the stairs and had stopped to catch their breath. From underneath his door came wafting in the foulest, most pungent stench of fresh shit, just like the time when he'd stepped in it in his living room. Or the curry-infused turd he'd dumped into the guy's mouth. He coughed and gagged, sitting upright, frantically searching for his switchblade under the pillow.

"Who the fuck is there?" he growled.

Then what sounded like someone pissing against the wall outside, a hissing sound, someone walking in something wet and squidgy. Slowly, the door opened of its own accord. Keith gripped the knife, ready to cut another throat, perform another autopsy on someone. The panting was louder now, two folks really getting into it. He wished Basher was here. He'd feed the fucker to the dog again. And for a second, he was convinced it was Basher he was looking at as it came into view. The idea that he was suffering a guilt-induced nightmare returned because the thing he was looking at could not possibly be real.

It was a dog. Or at least it looked like some kind of canine, but the thing was fucking huge, the size of a small pony. It reminded him of the werewolf in *An American Werewolf in London*, a fucking savage monster with teeth like a sabre-toothed tiger, dripping blood and glistening with saliva. Keith felt hugely insignificant with the knife in his hands. He could feel his cock shrivelling, trying to bury its way out of trouble.

"Fuck off," he said, in a voice not nearly as threatening as he would have liked. The dog growled.

The thing was covered in matted fur, brown and blotchy, stuck together in clumps as though it had been rolling around in mud. Then, the stench of fresh shit still permeating the air, coming at him in waves so thick he thought he could actually see it, he realised it may not be mud after all. Something brownish dripped from its long tongue as well. It took a step forward into the room, the small lamp beside Keith's bed making it easier to see. And there was something very wrong with this creature. Two things, actually that also enhanced Keith's idea he was dreaming.

First, the thing appeared to be semi-transparent, like a ghost; he could see the wall through its thick hide, but secondly and more importantly, were its eyes. While the creature was most definitely canine in shape and appearance, or wolfish, its eyes that gleamed in the semi-dark of Keith's room, were human. It was some kind of fucking human/dog hybrid. The thing glared at Keith, but there was also a twinkle in its eyes as though privy to some important knowledge that only it could possibly know.

"You fuck off, I said. I'll fuckin' cut your eyeballs out. And I mean it."

The thing ignored the threat and advanced closer until it was at the foot of the bed. Instinctively, Keith drew his legs up to his chest. Then it raised one huge paw, claws like a bear, onto the bed, then the other, never once taking its eyes from Keith. And Keith recognised those eyes. He'd seen them staring up at him while its owner slowly died a most brutal of deaths. This finally convinced him he was dreaming. It didn't make things any easier on his nerves, though.

Then the thing was on top of the bed, the springs pinging as its mammoth weight threatened to smash it. Keith could smell its breath, foul and repugnant, as if it had been eating someone's shit for the last hour, lapping it up. Then another two things occurred simultaneously, reinforcing Keith's wish for this to be some outrageous nightmare—it had to be.

"Hello, Keith. Did you miss me?"

A human's voice. *That* guy's voice. The one who had been fed to Basher and the Rottweiler. It came out as a growl but Keith definitely heard it right. The second thing to make Keith's balls shrivel and for his heart to leap up to his throat was when he saw the enormous, fat appendage between its legs. The extremely hard, fat and long appendage that glistened at its tip, dribbling pre-cum onto the bed. It sizzled as it hit the sheets.

"Fuck off," said Keith. "This is a dream, you're not real. I'm gonna wake up any second."

"Funny you should say that; I was thinking the exact same thing while your dogs were eating me, or before when you was fucking me. If it had stayed at that—you just fucking me then leaving—I might even have fantasised about it later, but nope. You know what it's like to be eaten to death? I used to wonder what it would be like to be fucked to death. Can you imagine? Being fucked so hard it caused a heart attack or something? I've been thinking about that a lot."

Keith lashed out at it—him—with his knife. The blade went straight through it. The thing chuckled. "You can't hurt me anymore, Keith, but I can certainly hurt you."

Then, with its paws it grabbed hold of Keith's legs and in one quick motion, brought them up and over Keith's head, locking them underneath. As someone who normally always slept naked, Keith's hairy arse was on a rather un-proud display. He tried to unlock his legs, his chest now heavy and compressed with this act of contortionism but found it impossible. As though they were tied behind his head. The thing crept closer, its heavy paws on his stomach, pressing down. The creature's cock was now so engorged, so long and fat it was longer than its whole body, an impossible

60

achievement. It dragged on the sheets leaving a slimy trail of pre-cum.

"Get away from me. You're not real." He lashed out again, cutting through thin air. The thing chuckled, like a dog with a sore throat. It drew yet closer and ran a rough tongue like sandpaper over Keith's face. Saliva dripped into Keith's eyes making them blurry. He didn't need his vision to feel what happened next, though. There was a dull ache as something pressed itself into Keith's arse. He squirmed, trying to free himself, grimacing as he felt his hole open up. The thing's face was now directly above his, mere inches away, breath that stank of shit blowing into his. Saliva dripped into Keith's eyes and mouth. Keith was panting now, as though preparing himself for a memorable sex session, but instead because he was terrified. He could feel his hole expanding impossibly wide, to the point the skin cracked around it.

And still it opened further, like someone was trying to push their head up his arse. A warm, sticky substance soaked his back and he knew it was blood as his arsehole was torn open. This must be what it's like to have a baby, he thought, but without the anaesthetic or whatever they gave women. The thing's cock entered him, filling him, spreading his cheeks so much he could feel the flesh tear all around it. He tried to scream but now the thing was kissing him, its long, wet tongue groping around inside his mouth, canines digging in like blades, hot breath like fumes from hell.

And still it continued. He could feel something pushing through his intestines, a sensation of his organs being moved out of the way, his stomach visibly puffing out as though a nine-month pregnancy was reduced to mere seconds, growth immediate. Something tickled his throat, something lodged there as if he'd eaten a large chunk of meat and it was stuck. His breathing came in harsh, laboured gasps as his neck expanded violently, barely conscious now. And then it happened.

The thing tilted Keith's head back and from out of his mouth came the dog's thick, wet cock, the head glistening with multiple secretions. The dog licked it, like a dog licking its own balls and the real pain came.

The dog began to thrust back and forth, in and out, the tip of its cock appearing and disappearing like some giant, mutant worm poking its head in and out of its home. Blood and mucus and shit ran down Keith's chin. He had been impaled. Just as he impaled the guy with the broomstick now this thing was doing the same to him but so much more painfully. The dog panted, the bed rocked, the headrest banging against the wall as the dog thrust harder and harder, faster and faster. Terry's eyes looked into his and he winked.

Keith was going to pass out. This was no dream, this was real. The pain told him so. It was as if he had eaten enough for ten and his stomach was going to explode. His arse as if it already had, the puddle of blood underneath him testament. Then the dog began to pant faster, its claws digging into Keith's cheeks drawing blood there too. Saliva ran copiously into Keith's wide mouth, but then the dog clamped a paw over it, began to growl and whine and Keith's mouth was suddenly filled with a warm, sticky liquid that ran from his nostrils, poured out of his mouth despite being closed in rivers of sticky cum. He could feel it dribbling out of his ears, up into his brain. He was going to drown in the thing's cum, his eyeballs bulged, the thick substance pushing them out of their sockets.

"How does it feel now, Keith? You wanted the ultimate experience, you got it. Think you could do that to me and the other guy and get away with it? Well, the joke's on you. Do you like the taste of my cum? You wanna repeat? We could do a trio, like a see-saw. Up, down, in, out, both at the same time."

But Keith barely heard him. He was swimming in and out of consciousness while swimming in this creature's cum. All he had wanted to do was teach the guy a lesson for shitting on his living room floor, for fucking his dog. He didn't care if the guy was gay, or what he got up to in his own time—that was all irrelevant. Someone in prison once told him that if you can't beat them, join them, and that was certainly true now. He had tried to show Terry he was the tough guy, that no one messed with him or his dog, and it had backfired on him. He wondered if dogs went to Hell too and what they got up to down there. Considering the circumstances, he thought he might enjoy it. Maybe he'd find Basher down there and they could carry on where Terry had left off. Such a strange world, he thought. Who knew how one might turn out.

The dog slowly pulled out what felt like a tree in there and removed its paw from Keith's mouth. Like an overflowing drain, thick, sticky liquids poured out bubbling and frothing running up Keith's nostrils, too thick to run back out again. Keith lay there dead, in a pool of filth, his intestines hanging out of the enormous hole where his arse used to be.

The dog howled like a wolf and slowly faded away. This time he really had been man's best friend.

The End

Grab your free book by signing up to my mailing list!
https://dl.bookfunnel.com/b00dfjcobx

Author's note

As I mentioned at the beginning, this story was based on a real event. Can you guess the scene? I assume so! It happened about 30 years ago at a small seaside town called Blanes near Barcelona before I moved to the city. My then boss used to run a bar as well as a large restaurant where he lived. To make things easier for himself and his wife who ran the bar (and at weekends his son, daughter, and daughter-in-law) he rented a bungalow which was halfway between the bar and his restaurant, often sleeping over to catch up on sleep. At the front of the bungalow was a large builder's merchants with lorries, trucks and builders coming in at all hours of the day. Behind the bungalow was the field as described. What happens in this story from that moment on, is exactly as it played out in real life. After we caught him in the act, we never saw him again.

So that got me thinking all these years later when I started writing. How could I use that in a story? I don't read or write extreme stories (although those that have read my Undead Possession series seem to disagree) and then it occurred to me a few weeks ago. Being unemployed and at home all day has one small benefit; I can get a lot of writing done. At the time of writing this, I have 7 novels sitting here in my files waiting to be published while I write the next. So I thought, why not try something different? I could use that experience to have a go at extreme horror which has seen an upsurge in popularity lately and from what I've seen of some of it, this story you have just read might even be considered tame!

So there you have it. Done! I hope you enjoyed this rather naughty little tale. If so, a review on Amazon and Goodreads is much appreciated, of course! It all helps to gain a little visibility. If you didn't like it, then I apologise here and now. I'm not sure if I'll write anything like this again. I guess it depends on the feedback I receive, for good or bad. So I'll leave that for you to decide…

Also by Justin Boote

Novels:

Serial
Carnivore
The Ghosts of Northgate
A Mad World

Short Story Collections:

Love Wanes, Fear is Forever
Love Wanes, Fear is Forever: Volume 2
Love Wanes, fear is Forever: Volume 3

The Undead Possession Series of Novels:

Book 1: Infestation
Book 2: Resurrection
Book 3: Corruption
Book 4: Legion
Book 5: Resurgence

Short Stories: (On Godless.com)

If Flies Could Fart
Grandma Drinks Blood
Badass
A Question of Possession

Printed in Great Britain
by Amazon

45855202R00040